B

Chicago Treasure

Chicago Treasure

by Larry Broutman, Rich Green, and John Rabias

BROUTMAN
PHOTOGRAPHY
B

Larry Broutman PHOTOGRAPHY, TEXT, AND CONCEPT

Rich Green ILLUSTRATION AND TEXT

John Rabias DIGITAL EFFECTS

Design, production, editing, and text contribution **Carol Haralson**

PUBLISHED BY

BROUTMAN PHOTOGRAPHY, LLC

106 W. GERMANIA PLACE, SUITE 207
CHICAGO, ILLINOIS 60610

DISTRIBUTED BY

LAKE CLAREMONT PRESS: A CHICAGO JOINT

AN IMPRINT OF EVERYTHING GOES MEDIA, LLC

www.everythinggoesmedia.com

Front cover: Melissa Ramirez as Old Mother Goose,
with Kaydence Guzman and Adriana Ramirez.
Back Cover: See caption on page 54. *Frontispiece:* Jesse Rosenthal at The Bean.
Facing: Jahon Gillespie as Wee Willie Winkle.

To my wife, Susan, who has been at my side through
good times and bad — fortunately, mostly good!

LARRY BROUTMAN

Introducing Chicago Treasure

Afterthoughts, Thanks, and Index

WHAT'S INSIDE

Just Imagine!

Kids Visit
the Land of Story,
Where Everything Imagined
Is Real.

starts on page 102

Now Showing!

Special Museum Exhibition:
The Kid Steps into
the Picture!

starts on page 126

Sightings!

Kids and Critters
Show Up Around Town.

Introducing Chicago Treasure

LARRY BROUTMAN

We speak of Chicago Treasure, but what is it? we ask.

You say the answer's simple, you're up for the task.

Is it the museums or the aquarium or the planes at O'Hare?

Or the Magnificent Mile displaying its wares?

If not, you ask, What can it be?

The theaters? Willis Tower? There's so much to see!

Is it the parks with the playgrounds, the beaches bathed in sun?

The paths for biking or the parks for a run?

Or the change of the seasons from summer to fall?

No. It is the children, greatest treasure of all.

— *Sandy Horwitz and Larry Broutman*

What a thrill! Finally done with all of the hard work: photography, Photoshop magic, illustrations, writing, and now it is all in the hands of our incredible book designer and poet, Carol Haralson. It is time to compose the introduction.

How did the idea of photographing children and showing them as characters in nursery rhymes and fairy tales originate? I started *Chicago Treasure* planning to follow the concept for my book *Chicago Unleashed*, which featured unexpected animals in iconic Chicago locations, except that this time I would photograph children and (with the help of our Photoshop guru John Rabias) place them in unlikely Chicago venues. Then, one morning, I awoke with a different idea: What if, when we photographed the children, we invited them to imagine themselves as the lovable storybook characters you will see in the pages of this book? A brain wave researcher at the MIT Media Lab has discovered that some of our most creative thoughts occur at the moment we fall asleep and while we are dreaming. I believe this is what occurred in my case. I realized that to make this dream happen I would need to find an artist experienced in illustrating children's books. How lucky was I to seek advice from John Rabias, who teaches at the School of the Art Institute of Chicago. He introduced me to Rich Green, who had just finished one of his Photoshop courses, and thus began our collaboration. It was clear from the very first illustration that an amazing journey lay before us. We invented the process as we went along. First we would discuss the children's story or rhyme to be illustrated. Rich would suggest possible poses, and I would photograph the children. Then Rich would create the illustration that merged the two.

A seven-foot-tall model lighthouse, decorated by Rich Green with images from *Chicago Treasure,* was among fifty-one custom lighthouses displayed by The Chicago Lighthouse for the Blind on Chicago's Magnificent Mile in summer 2018.

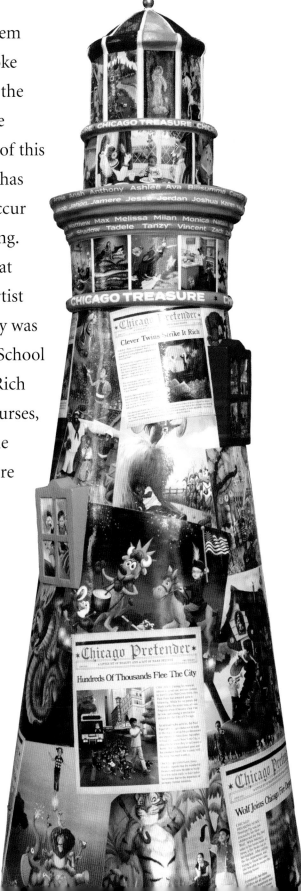

The children ranged in age from less than a year old (Humpty Dumpty) to nearly seventeen (Sleeping Beauty). Many were related to neighbors, friends, and relatives. Thank you all. A large number of the children were attending the Judy and Ray McCaskey Preschool Program at The Chicago Lighthouse for the Blind and Visually Disabled. The program is a free, full-day preschool curriculum offered through the Chicago Public Schools Preschool for All initiative. To be eligible, children must meet certain CPS requirements. The program offers a blended learning environment where children with and without visual impairments learn in a common setting. Such interaction and play instills sensitivity and respect for diversity from a young age. In this book we make no attempt to distinguish children who have visual and other disabilities from those who do not. In fact, a major theme throughout the book is inclusion.

There were many tender and delightful moments while posing the children. I particularly liked the questions they asked. Some inquired whether their picture in the book would make them famous. I sure hope so! One day, I received a call from Lee Burkland, principal of the McCaskey Preschool, who told me of the friendship between a new student who was blind, Rachelle Norington-Reaves, and a thoughtful boy, Camren Mickles, who was so sensitive to her needs that whenever she was standing or walking he held her hand and guided her. Within a few weeks, I was at the preschool to photograph the two, and they became our Jack and Jill. After meeting Rachelle and feeling her squeeze my hand, I spent the next few days composing this poem.

Being Blind

Although I'm blind and cannot see,
I ask you not to pity me.
I hear sounds, much more than you,
and with my Braille, I read well too.

I am free to walk wherever I may.
My guide dog helps me find the way.
And when he needs a rest, you see,
I have my trusty cane with me.

Sometimes I wonder what sky blue means,
or even the difference between reds and greens.
I wonder about the flowers too,
and the animals in our city zoo,
the tall buildings and the traffic lights,
or maybe how a bird takes flight.

But I am happy and loved and able to walk free.
So I ask you not to pity me.
No reason for you to pity me.

— *Sandy Horwitz and Larry Broutman*

On another photo shoot at the preschool, we photographed twins for
Popeye and Olive Oyl. When Ashlee Moore (aka Olive Oyl) changed into her
costume, she couldn't stop twirling to watch her skirt spin around.

One of the most endearing photo shoots took place at the home of the
Alfano family. The wheelchair belonging to Anthony (aka King Cole) became a
beautiful throne befitting a king. The love of Deanna and Tony Alfano filled the
home. Deanna's poem "Hello!" expresses so well this loving and caring.

Hello!

My name is Anthony.
Come close and you will see
there is nothing wrong with me!
No need to stare, it's just a chair.
It lets me move without a care.
It started with a boo-boo on my brain.
And, yes, the strength is hard to gain.
My arms are tight and my trunk is floppy,
and when I draw it's kinda sloppy.
I have this thing I call my "ears" —
It's only an aid but helps me hear.
I use a device to help me speak,
because my muscles are kinda weak.

I like to use it to tell you my name,
or ask you if you'll play a game.
I love to swim, read books, see sports on TV,
perhaps you'd like to do that with me?
Sometimes I feel left out
when I see kids run and shout,
but there is something I know without doubt:
Though my head may be hard to lift,
I know each day is a cherished gift.
And though I spend much time in my chair,
what makes life worthwhile is loving care.

— *Deanna Alfano*

On June 29, 2018, my wife Susan and I were invited to attend the Preschool Commencement at the Chicago Lighthouse. A number of our models were graduating to kindergarten. What a fun event. I was even asked to be one of the commencement speakers. With the parents of the children I had photographed in attendance, I had a chance to thank them for allowing us to present their children in this book. The joy that loving parents expressed at seeing their children become Chicago Treasures makes all of our work incredibly rewarding.

Commencement Day, Chicago Lighthouse Preschool, 2018.

Just Imagine!

Kids Visit the Land of Story, Where Everything Imagined Is Real.

Chicago Pretender

★ · SINCE 2018 · A LITTLE BIT OF REALITY AND A LOT OF MAKE BELIEVE ONE DOLLAR ★

COMICS

AND GAMES

HELP!

POW!!!

METROPOLIS –
After the commissioner put out the signal, our heroes sprang into action, protecting our fine city from villainous forces and saved the day. We asked for comment, to which they replied, "It's just all in a day's work."

```
S B V C S R U B A S
U R K I D A M S E L
P U Z U L B A M L R
E C J J D L T D E J
R E N J A S A P N L
M E Q N E T A I F H
A Q G O X R W U N C
N I R Q C O D H I L
S E V S P N V E F A
H A Y Z E G P L L R
B K M F A S T P Y K
S Q Q A B A T M A N
```

SUPERMAN	BATMAN	SIGNAL
HELP	DAMSEL	POW
BAM	VILLAIN	CLARK
BRUCE	SKYSCRAPER	FLY
FAST	STRONG	HEROES

★ Chicago Pretender ★

A LITTLE BIT OF REALITY AND A LOT OF MAKE BELIEVE

· SINCE 2018 ·   ONE DOLLAR

There's No Place Like Home

EMERALD CITY, OZ – Dorothy Gale made quite an entrance here in Oz the other day. She crash landed her house right into the middle of Munchkinland, much to the delight of the mayor, as in the process she freed the town from the terrible Witch of the East. As a reward, the Munchkins gave her the witch's ruby red slippers and sent her off to see the Wizard who could help her get back home to Kansas. As you might imagine, the Wicked Witch of the

West was infuriated when she learned of this news and set out to get Dorothy and her little dog too!

Dorothy took the yellow brick road out of Munchkinland towards the Emerald City. Along the way, she met up with a friendly Scarecrow who joined her in hopes the Wizard could give him a brain. They came across a rusty Tin Man who, after a little oiling, joined them in hopes of getting a heart. The last to come along was a Cowardly Lion in need of some courage.

At the time they did not know it, but they had everything they needed already and went on to save Oz from the Wicked Witch of the West. The Wizard rewarded them all, and they were last seen skipping down the yellow brick road celebrating. Our reporter was right there to photograph the scene. As much fun and adventure as they all had, Dorothy knew she needed to return home but promised she would never forget the friends she made while in Oz.

Previous page: Alex Jakopin and Zach Rodgers as Batman and Superman.

16

Ally Peek as Dorothy with her friends on the Yellow Brick Road.

The Princess and the Frog

A princess met a talking frog
while walking near the lily bog.
Kiss me, he said. Oh, kiss me, he cooed.
So the kind princess, not to be rude,
gave him a peck and set him down,
and he sprang up a prince in a gilded crown!

Little Boy Blue

Little Boy Blue, come blow your horn.
The sheep's in the meadow, the cow's in the corn.
Where is the boy who cares for the sheep?
Under a haystack, fast asleep.
I'll not wake him, no, not I, he is dreaming he can fly
to faraway places where someday he'll go,
over cities and oceans through clouds all aglow.

Prima Williams as the princess.

18

Zaven Chambers as Little Boy Blue.

★Chicago Pretender★

A LITTLE BIT OF REALITY AND A LOT OF MAKE BELIEVE

· SINCE 2018 · ONE DOLLAR

Wolf Joins Chicago Fire Department

CHICAGO
– Breaking News –
While Penelope Pig was baking a cake in her home made of straw, a fire broke out in her kitchen.

Fortunately, her three children are all members of the fire department, and they arrived at her house in seconds.

They brought with them the newest addition to the department, the Big Bad Wolf. When the wolf was younger, he used to blow down pig houses while singing, "I'll huff and I'll puff and I'll blow your house down." Now, the wolf has more fun working with the fire department, where he can blow out all the fires he wants, while singing, "I'll huff and I'll puff and I'll blow the fire out."

Moral of the story: More fun to be a Good Wolf than a Big Bad Wolf.

Salvador Zacarias as the Big Good Wolf.   21

✦ Chicago Pretender ✦

· SINCE 2018 · **A LITTLE BIT OF REALITY AND A LOT OF MAKE BELIEVE** ONE DOLLAR

It's Always Time for Tea

WONDERLAND – C. Cat reports that the Mad Hatter and March Hare welcomed an unexpected guest recently at their endless tea party. He saw Alice join them around six o'clock, but admits that among all the madness he was unsure whether she ever had tea herself.

The pair entertained her with riddles, none of which had answers, and they all changed places around the table from time to time. At one point, a dormouse awoke and shared a story with the group.

But things just kept getting curiouser and curiouser, so Alice politely excused herself from the table and continued on her way. She didn't want to be late for her game of croquet with the queen.

Emmy Peek as Alice.

★ Chicago Pretender ★

A LITTLE BIT OF REALITY AND A LOT OF MAKE BELIEVE

· SINCE 2018 ·   ONE DOLLAR

Prince Announces His Search Is Over

ROYAL KINGDOM – Just before midnight, a royal decree was issued stating that Prince Charming has found his Cinderella.

The prince has spent the past several months searching for the special girl whose foot fits into the magical glass slipper. A local young lady must have a fairy godmother looking out for her. When she tried on the slipper, it fit her perfectly, much to the prince's delight. Chicagoans everywhere rejoiced when they heard the news.

When asked for a comment, Cinderella's stepsisters stormed off and were later seen outside the palace crying hysterically. While palace officials did confirm that a wedding is in order, they would not yet give out a date.

In related news, the sales of women's shoes have skyrocketed, with many ladies now believing that a new pair of shoes really can change their lives!

Maritza Cervantes as Cinderella.

25

★ Chicago Pretender ★

A LITTLE BIT OF REALITY AND A LOT OF MAKE BELIEVE

· SINCE 2018 ·   ONE DOLLAR

Young Boy Climbs Beanstalk

THE ENGLISH COUNTRYSIDE – One of our foreign correspondents, Sandy Horwitz, filed this incredible story.

Jack Miller, on one of our rare sunny days, was out flying his kite in the pasture when his mother called him in. She tearfully asked Jack to take the family's only cow to town and sell her, as the family desperately needed money. On the way to town, Jack was tricked by a con man into selling the cow for a handful of what he called magic beans. His mother was distraught when he returned home with nothing but a few beans. Jack, undaunted, planted them in the yard. The next day, a huge beanstalk had sprouted from the earth.

Jack, known as a fearless boy, decided to climb the stalk to see where it might take him. High, high above, he came upon a giant eating his supper, and the giant had a goose at his feet. The giant told Jack that his goose could lay golden eggs.

Hearing this, Jack grabbed the goose and started to run with it, all the while the giant chasing behind him yelling, "Fee-fi-fo-fum!" Barely escaping the giant's grip, Jack slid down the beanstalk with the goose. Then he cut down the beanstalk and took the goose to his mother. When the goose began to lay eggs, they were indeed made of gold! The family never went hungry again, and all lived happily ever after.

Zach Rodgers as Jack.

Chicago Pretender

· SINCE 2018 · A LITTLE BIT OF REALITY AND A LOT OF MAKE BELIEVE ONE DOLLAR

Bears Sighted in North Woods

NORTH WOODS, WI – *The Pretender* just received word from a Mr. and Mrs. I. M. Bright that their daughter, Goldilocks, arrived home safely from an amazing adventure in Wisconsin.

While on a family camping trip, she wandered away and became lost in the North Woods. She claims that she came across a beautiful house deep in the woods and insists it was the home of three bears.

She also states that because of her long journey, she fell asleep in a bed belonging to the baby bear. She claims that she was awakened by Mama, Papa, and Baby Bear and became so frightened that she ran out of the house and didn't even thank the bear family for the delicious porridge snack she found in their kitchen.

Neveah Woods as Goldilocks.

Chicago Pretender

★ Chicago Pretender ★

· SINCE 2018 · A LITTLE BIT OF REALITY AND A LOT OF MAKE BELIEVE ONE DOLLAR

Missing Children Found Safe

BLACK FOREST, GERMANY –
Two young children who went missing in the woods have been found!

Having fallen upon hard times, Hansel and Gretel's parents had taken them camping in the woods, as Disney World was no longer an option. The pair had wandered off looking for firewood when they came across a house made entirely of candies, cookies, and other goodies that made their eyes open wide with excitement and their mouths water in anticipation.

Feeling hungry, but knowing it was not right to steal, the two took only one cookie to share between them. Then they knocked on the door and offered to trade Gretel's fine boots for the cookie. The woman who lived in the house was so impressed with the children's honesty that she refused the boots and helped them find their way back to their parents.

As a reward for the return of their children, the parents offered to help the elderly woman turn her gingerbread house into a business. The house is now a successful museum and candy store open for all to enjoy, and next year, all five plan to vacation together in Disney World.

Saige and Griffin Florsheim as Hansel and Gretel.

★ Chicago Pretender ★

· SINCE 2018 ·   **A LITTLE BIT OF REALITY AND A LOT OF MAKE BELIEVE**   ONE DOLLAR

Hermione Granger Saves the Day

FORBIDDEN FOREST – Harry Potter, Ron Weasley, and Hermione Granger recently avoided disaster while making their way through the forest near Hogwarts School.

Hermione is known to be an expert at spells. Well, most spells, that is. Unfortunately, the challenging Patronus is one she has had trouble with in the past. Fearing the danger that lurked ahead, Granger knew she might need to invoke it, as it is her most defensive charm. It was a great relief to all when she confidently declared, "Expecto Patronum" and her magical guardian otter appeared, protecting the group from a nearby Dementor.

Chloe Miller as the brave Hermione Granger.

★ Chicago Pretender ★

A LITTLE BIT OF REALITY AND A LOT OF MAKE BELIEVE
ONE DOLLAR

Local Boy Has Eggcellent Experience in England!

CHICAGO – A local couple and their one-year-old son, Jack, recently returned from a holiday abroad in England. While visiting the king's castle and grounds, they ran into none other than world famous Humpty Dumpty.

Mr. Dumpty, never known for being a tough egg to crack, immediately agreed to a photo opportunity and asked Jack to join him on his wall. Not wanting to be left out, one of the king's horses also hurried over to join in the fun.

Jack quickly climbed up, but only after his parents cautiously reminded Humpty not to fall!

Need a repair?
Let the
King's Men
put it back
together again!

Jack Linton as Humpty's buddy.

★ Chicago Pretender ★

| · SINCE 2018 · | A LITTLE BIT OF REALITY AND A LOT OF MAKE BELIEVE | ONE DOLLAR |

Mermaid Tells Whale of a Tale

UNDER THE SEA –
After breaking the spell cast by the awful sea witch, the Little Mermaid got her beautiful voice back. Upon her return home, all her friends from across the ocean came to hear her tell the tale of what had happened. Miss Puffer wanted to know how she broke the spell. Ollie the Octopus asked her to tell them all what life was really like on land. Hearts were aflutter, well, except for the Jellies', since they don't have hearts, wondering if she was going to marry the prince.

Then a huge reefside celebration began. Sharks were dancing with shrimp. An eel did the electric slide while a beluga played bass. Sea creatures large and small all continued to sing, swim, and dance the night away.

Everyone had a great time, although all that racket did make one resident a little crabby.

Malaya Harris as the Little Mermaid.

39

Little Arabella Miller

Little Arabella Miller
found a fuzzy caterpillar.
She gave him a home with a big glass view,
where he can chew and chew and chew.

Jackie Be Nimble

Jackie is nimble, Jackie is smart.
Her trampoline gave her a great head start.
She said to her friends, "Hold that candle high,
and I will clear it to reach the sky!"

Little Bo Peep

Little Bo Peep has playful sheep,
the silliest kind there are to keep.
They hide from her and slink away,
and laugh when she turns
and looks their way.

Jack and Jill

Jack and Jill went up the hill to fetch a pail of water.
The way was steep, the way was long,
but Jack helped Jill come after.
"I will be your eyes," he said. "I'll look out for us both."
And Jill was safe, for Jack is kind,
and that's what matters most.

Lexi Roth as Bo Peep.

43

Camren Mickles as Jack
and Rachelle Norington-Reaves as Jill.

★ Chicago Pretender ★

A LITTLE BIT OF REALITY AND A LOT OF MAKE BELIEVE

· SINCE 2018 ·   ONE DOLLAR

Muffet Says Spiders Are Friends

NORTHERN SUBURBS, CHICAGO – Investigative reporter Mrs. R. U. Sirius was recently sent on assignment to the home of the Muffets, a lovely young family with an incredible story. It turns out that their daughter, little Miss Natalie Muffet, has learned the language of spiders. She says that while her initial reaction was to be frightened away, she quickly realized that spiders could be friends. She claims to have trained a spider that came alongside her to sing and dance. Natalie pointed out that most of us have two left feet when it comes to dancing, so imagine teaching someone with eight!

The next time a spider sits down beside you, please do not step on him or swing at him with a rolled-up *Chicago Pretender*. Instead, Miss Muffett suggests introducing yourself, as she is doing in this photo that has become an instant hit all over the web!

44   Natalie Hubert as Little Miss Muffet.

★ Chicago Pretender ★

· SINCE 2018 ·   A LITTLE BIT OF REALITY AND A LOT OF MAKE BELIEVE   ONE DOLLAR

This Boy Is Grand

SOUTHERN INDIA – We have been reporting for several weeks now on an increasing number of tiger sightings and related incidents in the nearby jungle. Just yesterday, a local boy called Little Sam was out walking in the jungle with his sister. Perhaps it was the beautiful and bold colors of the new outfits their mother had made for them that caught the tiger's eye. He approached them smacking his lips as if to eat Little Sam up.

Thinking quickly, Little Sam offered the tiger his beautiful green umbrella. The tiger walked around a bit with the umbrella boasting loudly that he was the grandest tiger in all the jungle.

Then he stopped, slyly looked at Little Sam, and said, "I am going to eat up your sister." Little Sam was not going to let that happen, so he offered the purple and red shoes given to him by his father. At first, the tiger laughed,

saying, "What good are those to me when I have four paws and you have only two shoes?" But clever Sam suggested the tiger could wear them on his ears.

The tiger placed the shoes on his ears and again declared himself grandest of all. Hearing this bragging echoing throughout the jungle, other tigers appeared to challenge the statement. They all began running in a circle, trying to outdo one another. They ran so long and so fast they melted into butter.

Little Sam gathered up his umbrella and his shoes and collected the butter to bring home to his parents. His mother made a big batch of buttered pancakes to celebrate her son's quickness and good care of his sister.

Villagers have been stopping by all day to offer Sam their thanks for making the jungle a little bit safer once again.

Ansh Capoor and Aanchal Capoor as Sam and his sister.

Jack Sprat

Jack Sprat could eat no fat.
His wife could eat no lean.
So a hungry young man joined in the fun
to lick the platters clean.

Tommy Tucker

Tommy Tucker's Trio is a howling success.
They play on the sidewalk and take requests.
They croon for their supper and are well fed
on steak and gravy and butter and bread.

Kingston Burton as the hungry young man.

Layla Barrett applauding the tuneful Tommy Tucker.

Mary, Mary

Mary, Mary, dear little Mary,
how does your garden grow?
With birds and bees and butterflies
and smiling roses all in a row.

Yankee Doodle

Yankee Doodle went to town
wearing his tricorn hat.
An eagle led, a turkey piped.
A drummer played rat-a-tat-tat!

Hannah Greenburg as Mary.

Camillo Paz Vasquez as Yankee Doodle.

Young Dame Hubbard and Her Clever Dog

Young Dame Hubbard
went to the cupboard
to give the poor dog a bone.
But when she got there,
the cupboard was bare.
And so the poor dog had none.

She took a clean dish
to get him some tripe.
When she came back
he was smoking his pipe.

She went to the tavern
for white wine and red.
When she came back,
the dog stood on his head.

She went to the fruiterer's
to buy him some fruit.
When she came back,
he was playing a flute.

She went to the tailor's
to buy him a coat.
When she came back,
he was riding a goat.

She went to the hatter's
to buy him a hat.
When she came back,
he was feeding her cat.

She went to the barber's
to buy him a wig.
When she came back,
he was dancing a jig.

She went to the cobbler's
to buy him some shoes.
When she came back,
he was reading the news.

The Dame made a curtsy,
the dog made a bow.
The Dame said, "Your servant."
The dog said, "Bow-wow."

This wonderful dog
was Dame Hubbard's delight.
He could read, he could dance,
he could sing, he could write.
She gave him rich dainties
whenever he fed,
and pillows and cushions
to make up his bed.

Based on the 1804 version of an old English rhyme.
Zya Henson as Young Dame Hubbard.

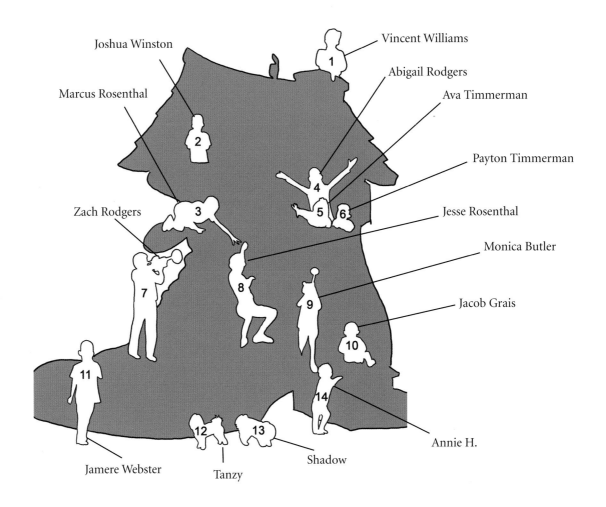

Joshua Winston

Vincent Williams

Marcus Rosenthal

Abigail Rodgers

Ava Timmerman

Payton Timmerman

Zach Rodgers

Jesse Rosenthal

Monica Butler

Jacob Grais

Annie H.

Jamere Webster

Shadow

Tanzy

The Old Woman Who Lived in a Shoe

There was once an old woman who lived in a shoe.
She had so many children she didn't know what to do.
They all loved music, so she started a band.
They sang and they danced and they did a headstand.
Some were acrobatic, some tossed a ball.
One did an imitation of a little talking doll.
They were so entertaining that people paid to see them,
and so the old woman could buy lovely food to feed them.

54

★ Chicago Pretender ★

· SINCE 2018 ·   A LITTLE BIT OF REALITY AND A LOT OF MAKE BELIEVE   ONE DOLLAR

Paul and Babe Head West

WYOMING – Reports are coming in from across the country that giant lumberjack Paul Bunyan and his trusty sidekick, Babe the Blue Ox, are on the move west.

Trackers have spotted larger-than-life footprints in the snow all over Minnesota. One of them proclaimed that by the time the snow melts, those footprints are sure to turn into 10,000 lakes!

Always a friend to lumberjacks and loggers, Paul dug by hand what is being called the Missouri River. Logs now float, with ease, down the river to the mills.

After all their hard work, Paul and Babe took a break to play in the flatlands of Wyoming. Wait, did we say flatlands? Well, not anymore. The duo started roughhousing, and when the dust and rock settled, the Grand Tetons were left

behind. As you might imagine, making mountains can get a bit messy, and Paul was overheard saying it was time to wash up. So he built himself a giant shower, which locals are calling Yellowstone Falls.

Our sources report that Paul is looking to get married and wants some baby Bunyans to help him develop Alaska. Good luck, Paul.

Bilisumma Bado as Paul Bunyan.

Peter Pan

With fairy dust from Tinkerbelle
and a demo from Peter Pan,
Wendy and her brothers
flew off to Neverland.

Zach Rodgers as Peter Pan and Abigail Rodgers
as Tinkerbelle.

Mary Had a Little Lamb

Mary had a little lamb
who followed her to school.
The lamb quickly learned her ABC's
and everyone thought she was cool.

Lila Roth as Mary, with the lamb playing herself.

Little Jack Horner

Little Jack Horner sat in a corner
eating a yummy pie. He stuck in his thumb
and pulled out a plum,
and said, "What a good boy am I!"

Salvador Zacarias as Little Jack Horner.

Peter, Peter, Pumpkin King

Peter, Peter, Pumpkin King,
liked to share most everything.
Indeed, he was a splendid host.
His friends loved pumpkin pie the most.

Jack Linton as the hospitable Peter.

★ Chicago Pretender ★

A LITTLE BIT OF REALITY AND A LOT OF MAKE BELIEVE

· SINCE 2018 ·   ONE DOLLAR

Hundreds of Thousands Flee the City

CHICAGO – Putting his musical talents to good use, and not content to merely play *Hot Cross Buns*, this Pied Piper has amassed quite a following. While his rat parade did block traffic for some time, all was forgiven when it became clear that he was performing a spectacular service for the City of Chicago.

An animal rights activist, the Pied Piper of Chicago chose not to walk to the waterfront as his predecessors are reputed to have done, but rather to lead the rats to New York City, a place he believes they'd feel more at home. With a determined gaze and his sneakers laced, the journey will be long, but well worth it.

Our Chicago contributor, Jenny Friedes, reports that the wonderful theaters will now be able to build a few extra stalls in their ladies' bathrooms due to the departure of so many former residents.

Logan Florsheim as the Pied Piper.

★ Chicago Pretender ★

A LITTLE BIT OF REALITY AND A LOT OF MAKE BELIEVE

· SINCE 2018 ·   ONE DOLLAR

Stories of Pinocchio Continue to Grow

SOMEWHERE OUTSIDE FLORENCE, ITALY – News is spreading fast that local woodcarver Mastro Geppetto has created such a lifelike marionette that neighbors are certain it is a real boy.

Before we here at the *Chicago Pretender* could report such a wild claim, we sent reporter Carlo Collodi to investigate. He said he was skeptical at first, fearing the locals were telling little white lies and exaggerations. But he now confirms the reports and said he could hardly believe his own eyes. The hand-carved pinewood puppet, who goes by the name Pinocchio, has learned to talk, walk, and even dance with no strings attached.

Carlo said that, much like any other young boy, Pinocchio gets into some mischief now and then. However, Mastro Geppetto has his ways of knowing if Pinocchio is telling the truth or not. For our young readers, please check the size of Mr. Pinocchio's nose.

64   Tadele Daniel as Pinnochio.

Young King Cole

Young King Cole is a very merry soul,
and a very merry soul is he.
He called for his pipe, he called for his bowl,
and he called for his fiddlers three.

Polly Put the Kettle On

Polly, put the kettle on,
we all would like some tea!
The parrots pour, the sugar plunks.
What a wonderful place to be.

Anthony Alfano as Young King Cole.　　　Laney Grunes as Polly.

Mary Poppins

Mary Poppins, the best of nannies,
could fly above the rooftops.
And when she was with the children,
life was love and lollypops.

Violet Kongabel as the beloved Mary Poppins.

Rain, Rain, Don't Go Away

Rain, rain, don't go away.
Come bring your puddles, we love to play.
We have our umbrellas for just such a day.
Rain, rain, please don't go away!

Layla Barrett and Aiden Richardson enjoying the rain.

★ Chicago Pretender ★

| · SINCE 2018 · | A LITTLE BIT OF REALITY AND A LOT OF MAKE BELIEVE | ONE DOLLAR |

Pea Trick Works Again

COPENHAGEN – Breaking News – After a long night traveling in the cold and rain, a penniless young girl came upon our castle and asked if she could stay the night. She claimed she was a princess (ha, ha) and desperately needed some rest. Our gracious king and queen readily welcomed her to stay, and their son, the prince, gave her something to eat as she warmed herself by the fire.

She was brought to a room, and shown a lavish stack of colorful mattresses. Seeing this setup, she was very excited to catch up on some much-needed beauty rest. The only problem was that she found herself tossing and turning all night long. She could not figure out why she could not get comfortable.

In the morning, the king and queen asked her how she had slept. She told them quite poorly, and said it was as if something was poking her side all night. Instead of being offended, the queen smiled in great delight. After seeing how well she had gotten on with the prince, the queen did the pea trick and placed the royal pea under the mattresses to determine if this young guest was in fact a real princess. Since she was sensitive enough to feel the pea, she had passed the test.

We expect a royal wedding announcement at any moment.

70   Abigail Rodgers as the princess.

★ Chicago Pretender ★

· SINCE 2018 · A LITTLE BIT OF REALITY AND A LOT OF MAKE BELIEVE ONE DOLLAR

Prince Rescues Rapunzel and Arrives at Chicago Lighthouse

CHICAGO – A young prince who hails from Chicago is being celebrated today as a local hero. After rescuing Rapunzel from her tower in Hungary, the prince and his trusty steed transported the lovely princess safely to the Chicago Lighthouse.

With the help of countless forest friends along the way, they made the more-than-seven-thousand-kilometer journey in record time.

When asked about his bravery, the modest young prince replied, "Rapunzel let down her hair, and I knew right away I could not fail her!"

Search still on for Dame Gothel

Matthew Jefferson as the prince.

★ Chicago Pretender ★

A LITTLE BIT OF REALITY AND A LOT OF MAKE BELIEVE

· SINCE 2018 ·   ONE DOLLAR

Pretender Reporter Saves Riding Hood

MICHIGAN — *Pretender* cub reporter Sandy Horwitz has been credited with saving Miss Red Riding Hood. While on vacation at her summer home in Michigan, Sandy noticed that a young girl in a red cape passed her home every day with a basket of goodies. Engaging the girl in conversation, Sandy discovered that she visited her grandmother each day and always brought her a gift in a basket. Sandy warned the girl about a big bad wolf living in the forest, but the girl was not afraid.

Sandy said yesterday, she followed the girl to her grandmother's house to make sure she was safe. The wolf had arrived there first and had locked the grandmother in a closet. Disguising himself as the grandmother, he opened the door and grabbed Riding Hood as she entered, threatening not only to eat the goodies in the basket, but also to eat her and the grandmother too! Sandy rushed in, punched the wolf in the stomach, and kicked him in the "you know where." The wolf fled, and Sandy is credited with rescuing both Riding Hood and her grandmother.

The *Pretender* is going to reward Sandy with an extra day off.

Dominika Tamley as Little Red Riding Hood.

Ride a Painted Horse

Children all gather along a green course
to see the fine lady on the painted horse.
With rings on her fingers and bells on her toes,
she will have music wherever she goes.

Layla Lawler as the lady. From left to right: Jamere
Webster, Jordan Ruiz McCleary, and Camren Mickles.

Rub-a-Dub-Dub

Rub-a-dub-dub, three men in a tub.
Who do you think they might be?
The butcher, the baker, the candlestick maker,
and all are gone to sea.

Max and Charlie Greenburg as the butcher and baker.

Sleeping Beauty

A king and queen had a girl-child they had wished for many a year.
They gave a joyful christening feast for guests from far and near.
Among them came seven good fairies, and each brought the baby a gift.
Wit, grace, goodness, and song — but then came a terrible rift!
An evil eighth fairy cast a curse on the girl.
A prick from a spindle would one day kill her.
The seventh good fairy, who'd yet to speak, tried to reverse the curse,
saying, no, not death, but sleep would come. Sleep, and nothing worse.

And it happened. Beauty slept a hundred years
after pricking her hand on a spindle.
Roses grew thick up the castle wall
and tumbled in the window.
The fairies kept watch and did not forsake her.
They knew her prince's kiss would wake her.

And then one day a kind, brave prince
who'd heard Beauty's story rode by.
He spied the hidden castle and climbed up through the vines.
He took her hand and kissed her cheek and heard her stir and sigh.
She was his one true love, he knew.
He'd forever be beguiled.
And Beauty awoke and opened her eyes
and looked at him and smiled.

Sara Main as Sleeping Beauty. Fairies playing themselves.

What's in a Name?

GERMANY – After a miller stretched the truth and said his daughter could spin straw into gold, the king asked to see this extraordinary girl. When she appeared at the castle, he locked her in a cellar with a spinning wheel and demanded she make gold for him. The poor child did not know what to do. But then out of nowhere appeared a chatty little goblin of a man who said he would turn the straw into gold in exchange for her necklace. Having no other choice, she agreed, and — like magic — straw began spinning into gold.

The next morning, the king was thrilled to see all his new gold, but he was greedy and demanded more. In the nights that followed, the ever-so-talkative goblin returned and spun gold in exchange for more of the girl's belongings. When she had nothing left to give him, he said he would keep spinning if she would promise him her first child. That was unless she could guess his name.

As he spun each night, the goblin chattered on and on about himself. The girl stayed awake and listened. Finally late one night, without realizing it, the goblin slipped and said his own name.

Years went by, and the girl's first child was born. When the smug goblin arrived to claim his prize, the miller's daughter greeted him. "How nice to see you, Mr. Rumpelstiltskin," she said, smiling.

For once the little goblin was totally speechless.

Milan Webb as the miller's daughter.

★ Chicago Pretender ★

· SINCE 2018 ·	A LITTLE BIT OF REALITY AND A LOT OF MAKE BELIEVE	ONE DOLLAR

Snow White Finally Awakens

GERMANY – Breaking News – The *Chicago Pretender* just received an exclusive update from our foreign correspondent Mr. Grumpy.

Several months ago, the magic mirror revealed that Snow White was the fairest in the land. Soon after, she fell into a deep sleep after biting into a poisoned apple given to her by none other than her jealous mother, the wicked queen of Fairytale Land.

We are excited to report that the handsome prince of Storyland, after spying Snow White in the forest, was able to wake her. Mr. Grumpy has also confirmed that Snow White and her prince are now married and living happily ever after.

Karen Hernandez as Snow White.

★ Chicago Pretender ★

· SINCE 2018 ·   A LITTLE BIT OF REALITY AND A LOT OF MAKE BELIEVE   ONE DOLLAR

A New Sheriff in Town

ANDY'S ROOM — A handsome and mysterious space ranger arrived recently, and our local sheriff was not too happy about it. We all know by now that Sheriff Woody likes to be in charge and that, like some little kids, he can have a bit of trouble sharing. As a matter of fact, he made a rootin' tootin' fuss about how the space ranger was not real, but just a toy.

The fearless space ranger, however, knows he is here on an intergalactic mission and set out to prove to his new roommates that he is in fact the real Buzz Lightyear. The only way to do that wass to show them his laser blaster and prove that he can fly. So he climbed high atop the post at the foot of Andy's bed and yelled "To infinity and beyond!" before taking his leap.

Cautious optimism turned to sheer delight as Buzz Lightyear's roommates recalled the moment they first witnessed him fly. Rex the Dinosaur said he "flew magnificently."
Bo Peep, Mr. Potato Head, and Slinky Dog described how the room erupted in applause.

Said the ever-reluctant Sheriff Woody, "That wasn't flying. It was falling with style."

Whatever it was, you have a friend in us, Buzz!

Aiden Richardson as Buzz Lightyear.

★ Chicago Pretender ★

| · SINCE 2018 · | A LITTLE BIT OF REALITY AND A LOT OF MAKE BELIEVE | ONE DOLLAR |

The Belle of the Ball

RIQUEWIHR, FRANCE – Once a small-town girl with her head in the clouds or a good book, Beauty stepped out as the *Belle* of the ball this past weekend in a stunning gold gown with hand-beading and sequins that was found in the wardrobe of the fashionable and often outspoken Madame de la Grande Bouche.

Much to everyone's surprise and delight, Beauty's date for the evening was the tall, dark, and mysterious Beast. We here at the *Pretender* have described the Beast in the past as somewhat coarse, certainly no Prince Charming. While he is still a little rough around the edges, he sure did clean up nicely for the evening.

When the pair took to the dance floor, it became clear to onlookers that there just might be something there between them. "The entire scene was so warm and enchanting," said the self-proclaimed romantic Monsieur Lumière.

Mrs. Potts and her son, Chip, said, "A few days ago they were barely even friends!"

Cogsworth, who only had a minute to speak with us, ventured that "Perhaps there is a little something there," but went on to say he was not ready to get his hopes up yet.

No one was willing to say much about the beautiful encased rose that could be seen glowing in the west wing of the castle. But there was a noticeable alarm from some when a petal softly fell from the rose. So we will certainly have to do a bit more investigating and report back in when we learn more.

In the meantime, word of the evening spread quickly through the quiet village. Gaston, who has notoriously expressed interest in Beauty, was not very happy about it. But then, as he always does, he just went on and on and on about himself.

Are Beauty and the Beast the new "It" couple? Only time or Cogsworth can tell!

Treasure Island

The pirate life holds more danger
than a treasure chest holds gold.
Young Jim Hawkins discovered this
when he shipped aboard.
When home at last, with his fair share,
he said he was happy to just stay there.

Tom Thumb

Imagine that you were the size of a thumb.
The things you'd have seen, the things you'd have done.
Ridden a locust past Waterhose Fall,
made friends with an ant where the flowers grow tall.
You'd see wonders and magic wherever you looked,
and they'd put your adventures in a storybook.

Christopher Edwards as Jim Hawkins.

Sean Rocquemore as Tom Thumb.

★ Chicago Pretender ★

A LITTLE BIT OF REALITY AND A LOT OF MAKE BELIEVE

· SINCE 2018 ·

ONE DOLLAR

The Ride of a Lifetime

CHICAGO – Reports have come in from children all around the world saying that they spotted a jolly old elf and his tiny reindeer flying way up in the sky. Some heard the jingle of bells first and then recognized the red glow of the lead reindeer's nose among the stars shining so brightly.

But there was something a bit different. Santa usually delivers presents on his own, but it appears that this year one lucky boy was selected to co-pilot the sleigh. The whirlwind trip ended here in Chicago when Santa dropped off the boy at home. When we reached out for comment, he reported that, "Santa let me hold the reigns, control the reindeer navigation system, and shout out Ho, Ho, Ho. It was awesome!"

The young man instantly became the envy of good little girls and boys everywhere. Internet search engines were overloaded with children looking for ways to apply for this coveted assignment next year. Even the naughty kids were reading up on how to get on the nice list before Santa checked it twice.

Vincent Williams as Santa's co-pilot.

★ Chicago Pretender ★

A LITTLE BIT OF REALITY AND A LOT OF MAKE BELIEVE

· SINCE 2018 · ONE DOLLAR

Who Will Olive Oyl Choose?

CHESTER, IL – Longtime *Chicago Pretender* contributor E. C. Segar reports to us that the boys are up to their old tricks again. Each of them is trying to outdo the other in their attempts to woo Olive Oyl. Ms. Oyl said she loves being the center of attention. What girl wouldn't like to be showered with flowers and gifts? Though she did mention she could do without all the fighting.

Bluto, who is charming, but a bit rough around the edges, would like nothing more than to take Olive away and sail the world. While Bluto may be a strong competitor, Popeye is no wimp and won't give up that easily. He is sure to flex his muscles to defend Olive and try to win her over. Meanwhile, little Swee'Pea once again tries to catch Olive's attention, but, as usual, he is not having much luck.

No one can say for sure who Olive will choose, but our money is on Popeye. After all, he is strong to the finish, 'cause he eats his spinach!

92 Ashlee Moore and Adonis Moore as Olive Oyl and Popeye.

The Girl in the Hoop

The showman in the spotlight
draws the eyes of the crowd below
to the girl in the hoop far, far above.
She's the star of the circus show.

Little Orphan Annie

Little Orphan Annie had many chores to do.
She climbed atop a washtub and belted out a tune.
Her friends supplied the chorus, and everyone had fun.
And when the show was finished, all the work was done.

MacKenzie Mitchell and Decklyn Mitchell
as the showman and the flying girl.

Annie H. as Little Orphan Annie.

★ Chicago Pretender ★

· SINCE 2018 ·   A LITTLE BIT OF REALITY AND A LOT OF MAKE BELIEVE   ONE DOLLAR

Twins Strike it Rich

PERSIA – Ever wish you could discover a cave full of golden treasure? Well, it appears that twins Ali and Alibaba have done just that.

On a recent trip to gather firewood, the twins happened to overhear a group of forty thieves chatting about a secret trove in a stone cave. The opening to the cave was sealed by magic, and only those who knew the password could open or close it. Listening further, they heard one of the thieves say the secret password. After the thieves left, they approached the cave entrance and together called out, "Open Sesame!"

Much to their surprise and delight, the stone blocking the entrance magically began to rise, revealing treasure and gold as far as their little eyes could see.

The clever pair knew they could only take small amounts at a time, so as not to tip off the thieves that anything was missing. They made several trips back to the cave, each time shouting out, "Open Sesame," and each time returning home with a handful of coins and jewels. The pair got so good at eluding detection that perhaps we should say this story is about forty-two thieves!

Ashlee Moore and Adonis Moore as Ali and Alibaba.

Pear Blossom and the Dragon

Lovely Pear Blossom lived with her mom
on water and crumbs that were nearly gone,
so she bravely offered to travel alone
to seek alms from her uncle, whose wealth was well known.

En route to the city, where she'd never been,
was a bright swath of red, a poppy-filled garden.
There two girls shouted and leapt near the gate
chasing a poor butterfly who tried to escape.

Pear Blossom rescued the delicate flyer
and released him to freedom, to the children's ire.
When the girls derided her, she explained her errand.
"The dragon," they said, "will be your end!"

Uncertain what to do, she sat beneath a tree.
Is there a dragon? she thought. *Will he be the end of me?*
Then Butterfly Fairy floated down into view.
"For your kindness," she said, "we will help you."

"The dragon loves flowers. Take this bouquet.
It will tame and delight him, you can go on your way."
Pear Blossom thanked her and walked with the flowers
to the gate of the city near the dragon's bower.

She presented her gift, and the dragon was pleased.
He allowed her to go, but first said, "Take these —"
and placed in her hands three fine strands of jewels.
"You understood me," he said. "These should be yours."

Chloe Wozniak as Pear Blossom.
Based on an old Chinese legend.

98

She walked through the city to her uncle's home,
but he sent her away, for his heart was stone.
Yet the empress heard the story of Pear Blossom's travail,
and she asked to see the mother and the mother's brave girl.

She was fond of them at once and invited them to stay.
They live happily in the palace until this very day.
And the dragon no longer scorches
the land with his fiery roar,
so the flowers he loves can flourish
and brighten his bower door.

★ Chicago Pretender ★

| · SINCE 2018 · | A LITTLE BIT OF REALITY AND A LOT OF MAKE BELIEVE | ONE DOLLAR |

Genie Behind Incredible Transformation

AGRABAH – Columnist Scheherazade shares a tale of a young local boy named Aladdin. Suddenly villagers claim they have seen the boy and their princess flying high above the city on what can only be described as a magic carpet. Reports have yet to be substantiated.

Some speculate Aladdin must have found the Mystical Lamp and released the all-powerful genie who is said to grant three wishes. What else can explain his sudden wealth, flashy new wardrobe, and that palace he is building for the princess?

According to Miss Scheherazade, there is much more to this developing story. She estimates it would take her 1,001 nights to tell the full tale. Come back tomorrow to learn more.

Tadele Daniel as Aladdin.

Now Showing!

Special Museum Exhibition:
The Kid Steps into the Picture!

Page 103: Millie Braude in *Højbro Plads* (High Bridge Square, Copenhagen, Denmark). Painting by Paul Gustave Fischer (1860–1934).

Left: Grace Conroy strolls a seaside path in *Homme Portant une Blouse*, 1884. Painting by Gustave Caillebotte (1848–1894).

Jesse Rosenthal with a snowball in *Vinterdage in Kongens Nytorv*. Painting by Paul Gustave Fischer (1860–1934).

Gunder D'hondt by the Seine
in *On the Banks of the River Seine*.
Painting by Jean Beraud (1848–1935).

Carlos Peña asks directions in *The Boulevard des Capucines and the Vaudeville Theater*, 1889. Painting by Jean Beraud (1848–1935).

Jean Béraud.

Brinton D'hondt on a Parisian boulevard
in *Church of San Philippe du Roule, Paris*.
Painting by Jean Beraud (1848–1935).

Jean Béraud.

Drew Bernstein as The Girl with the Striped Umbrella in *Le Modiste Sur Les Champs Elysee*, 1900. Painting by Jean Beraud (1848–1935).

Millie Braude on the bridge in *Le Pont de L'Europe*, 1876. Painting by Gustave Caillebotte (1848–1894).

Danielle Smith texts home from a Parisian bench
in *Boulevard de Capucines,* 1875.
Painting by Jean Beraud (1848–1935).

Francesca Pruger, Benjamin Pruger, and Theodore Slight-Sama
buy carrots and radishes in *Les Halles*. Painting by Paul Gustave Fischer (1860–1934).

Dalin Alexi and Light Ayli Dohrn read in *Les Oranges*, 1878. Painting by Gustave Caillebotte (1848–1894).

Kingston Burton and Pearl Hardigan in *Le Billard*, 1878. Painting by Jean Beraud (1848–1935).

Jack Foster Cunard with his bicycle
in *Jagtvej Toward Vibenhaus Runddel*.
Painting by Paul Gustave Fischer (1860–1934).

Ally Peek and her poodle in a French bakery
in *La Patisserie*, 1889.
Painting by Jean Beraud (1848–1935).

Chloe Wozniak in a yellow cap in *Automat*, 1927.
Painting by Edward Hopper (1882–1967).

Ruby Rosenthal up late
in *Nighthawks,* 1942.
Painting by Edward Hopper
(1882–1967).

Aria Wozniak watches
ladies chatting over tea
in *Chop Suey,* 1929.
Painting by Edward Hopper
(1882–1967).

Ruby Rosenthal visits an iconic couple
in *American Gothic*, 1930.
Painting by Grant Wood (1891–1942).

Max Greenburg at the train station
in *Breaking Home Ties*, 1954.
Painting by Norman Rockwell (1894–1978).

Max Greenburg at home plate
in *Construction Crew*, 1954.
Painting by Norman Rockwell (1894–1978).

Breanna and Calysta Dunworth and Howie
the cat help with the milk in *Early Light*.
Painting by Grant Wood (1891–1942).

Abigail and Zach Rodgers on a porch railing in *Sit a Spell*.
Painting by Grant Wood (1891–1942).

Chloe Wozniak helps in the garden in *In Full Bloom*.
Painting by Grant Wood (1891–1942).

Sightings!

Kids and Critters Show Up Around Town.

Page 127: *Cloud Gate* (aka The Bean), designed by Anish Kapoor, is comprised of 168 welded and polished stainless steel plates. Its highly relective surface encourages inventive poses. *Jesse Rosenthal loves to clown around in front of The Bean.*

Millennium Park was conceived by Mayor Richard M. Daley in 1997. Today it encompasses more than twenty acres of public space and is one of the most important tourist destinations in the city. Lurie Gardens, seen here, covers more than three acres and is partially surrounded by a fifteen-foot-high hedge. *Theodore Slight-Sama and Joshua Winston are escorted through Lurie Gardens by one of the park's cheetah families.*

Millennium Park's Jay Pritzker Pavilion was designed by the world-famous architect Frank Gehry. Its lawn and fixed seats can hold over 10,000 people. *Nylah Ash, a skilled runner, helps keep wild animals out of the pavilion during concerts.*

Yaacov Agam's totem-pole–like sculpture, titled *Communication X9,* is located across from the Chicago Cultural Center at the corner of Michigan Avenue and Randolph Street. *Emmy Peek, a professional pet walker, is often seen near the sculpture.*

The Bud Billiken Parade and Picnic has been held annually since 1929 in Chicago's Bronzeville/Washington Park neighborhood. The largest African-American parade in the United States, it is named after a fictional character created by the *Chicago Defender* newspaper. The focus of the parade is educating Chicago's youth. *Chicago Lighthouse preschoolers Nylah Ash, Karen Hernandez, Wynter Elliot, Matthew Jefferson, Joshua Winston, Vincent Williams, and Jamere Webster show off their agility and musical talents on a variety of wind instruments while marching in the parade.*

Within Millennium Park is the public space that contains The Bean, one of Chicago's most visited attractions. Here the city skyline reflects in its highly polished surface. *Sara Main, an expert panda trainer and walker, is often seen on the plaza.*

A bridge enthusiast's dream, Chicago has eighteen movable bridges spanning the Chicago River. The bridges are raised in the spring to allow sailboats access to Lake Michigan and in the fall to allow them access to their winter storage facilities. The State Street crossing was first bridged in 1864.

The current State Street Bridge was dedicated as a memorial for World War II veterans who fought in the Philippines. *Much to the dismay of the bridge tender, Chloe Wozniak, Aria Wozniak, and Max Logan jump across the bridge on the backs of their African impalas.*

Chicago has one of the most beautiful skylines in the world, showing off the elegant architecture of the city. *While zebras were not one of the animals originally planned to inhabit the lagoon area, Ruby and Jesse Rosenthal are brave enough to ride one across the water, a ride they will not soon forget.*

Soldier Field, seen here from Northerly Island, opened in 1924 and serves as a memorial to American soldiers who died in foreign wars. Since 1971, it has been the home of the Chicago Bears. *Camillo Paz Vasquez enjoys a bearback ride courtesy of the Bears' mascot.*

Pioneer Court on Michigan Avenue is a showplace for large sculpture. *Forever Marilyn,* by Seward Johnson, was displayed there. Over twenty-six feet tall, it represents Marilyn Monroe in her role in the movie THE SEVEN YEAR ITCH. *Shawn Peek and her daughter, Emmy, residents of bear country in Wisconsin, tour Chicago on their own black bear.*

Leo Vanek just got fitted for his new penguin suit at Chicago's Finest Penguin Clothing Store. His clever disguise has allowed him to tour the city with other penguins.

The Chicago Theater opened its doors in 1921. Its glowing marquee that reads C-H-I-C-A-G-O is nearly six stories tall and has become a symbol of State Street. The grandeur of the interior is breathtaking, complete with beautiful murals above the stage. *Leo Vanek and his penguin friends put on their formal attire to attend the film MARCH OF THE PENGUINS at the Chicago Theater.*

Navy Pier was built as a dock for freight and passenger traffic and a site for public events. During World War II, it was a navy training facility. Later, the University of Illinois at Chicago held classes there. It eventually became a world-class recreation center with parks, shops, restaurants, and family attractions that draws nine million human visitors each year. *Also some penguins, and fans of penguins, including Leo Vanek.*

The Museum of Science and Industry in Jackson Park was originally the Palace of Fine Arts for the 1893 World's Columbian Exposition. The museum has more than 2,000 exhibits displayed in seventy-five major halls. *Chloe Wozniak, a museum volunteer, offers a resident antelope a carrot.*

141

Horse racing, an equestrian performance sport, has a long and distinguished history. It has been practiced around the world since ancient times. In flat racing, the horses run on an oval track and races can vary in length from 400 meters up to two and a half miles. *Female jockeys are becoming more common, as shown by one of the youngest and best, Ruby Rosenthal, recent winner of the Kentucky Derby.*

The Chicago River Walk, on the south bank of the Chicago River, offers good views of the surrounding buildings. Particularly prominent on the north side of the river are the Wrigley Building and Tribune Tower. *Abigail Rodgers was recently seen on the bridge with a family of koala bears, who also like the views of downtown Chicago.*

Wrigley Field on Chicago's North Side has been home to the Chicago Cubs since its construction in 1916. Between 1921 and 1970, it also served as home to the Chicago Bears of the National Football League. Wrigley is known for its ivy-covered brick walls and the iconic red marquee over its main entrance. *Karen Hernandez rounding third base and heading for home! Will she make it?*

When the Cubs won the World Series in 2016, thousands of people photographed the marquee as it flashed WORLD SERIES CHAMPIONS. *Theodore Slight-Sama, Abigail and Zach Rodgers, and Benjamim "Benny" Pruger, with their parents' permission, climbed to the top of the sign.*

The Chicago Bears (originally called the Decatur Staleys) and the National Football League were founded by George Halas in 1920. The Staleys became the Bears in 1921 and began playing in Wrigley Field. Their current home is Soldier Field in Chicago. *Jesse and Marcus Rosenthal, season ticketholders and great cheerleaders, help celebrate a recent home victory.*

Chicago's Chinatown is not only a major tourist attraction, but a popular area for locals who want to enjoy shopping and a delicious Chinese meal. It is also home for over 70,000 Asian residents. *Aria and Chloe Wozniak celebrate the Year of the Tiger.*

The Baha'i House of Worship in Wilmette, Illinois, is the only one of its kind in the United States. Construction began in 1922, but the exterior of the building was not completed until 1943. The building is clad with a mixture of Portland cement and quartz and embellished with very intricate carved details that make it beautiful to view at any time of day. *Not wanting to interfere with visiting pandas, Max Greenburg whispers to his sister, Hannah, to stand up and tiptoe away on the count of three.*

Afterthoughts

RICH GREEN AND LARRY BROUTMAN

Preparing this book has been such a joyful experience for all associated with the project, particularly the children and their families. We know this joy will be magnified when the book is published. As we prepare some final thoughts, it is three years, or, to be exact, 1,093 days, from the time of our initial collaboration on the *Chicago Treasure* illustrations. The children who were photographed early in this journey are now two and three years older. Jesse and Marcus ("The Old Woman Who Lived in a Shoe") are quickly maturing and no longer "little kids," as can be seen in a photo taken in July 2018 (page 152).

During summer of 2018, The Chicago Lighthouse for the Blind and the City of Chicago celebrated the themes of access and inclusion by presenting fifty-one specially decorated model lighthouses along Chicago's Magnificent Mile. A number of them were painted by artists with visual and physical disabilities.

Susan and Larry Broutman sponsored one of the lighthouses, and Rich Green embellished it with illustrations created for this book. Many families whose children appear in our pages came to see their images on Michigan Avenue, The Magnificent Mile. What a perfect and joyful way to celebrate Chicago's true treasure and our impending publication.

Ava and Payton Timmerman proudly view themselves inside a shoe.

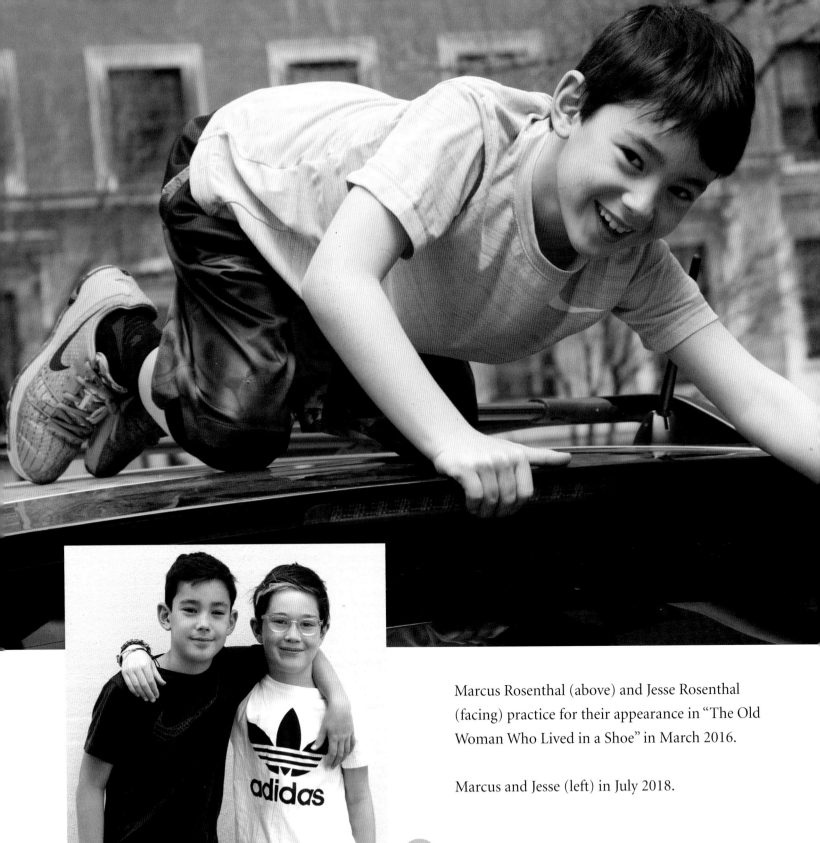

Marcus Rosenthal (above) and Jesse Rosenthal (facing) practice for their appearance in "The Old Woman Who Lived in a Shoe" in March 2016.

Marcus and Jesse (left) in July 2018.

Natalie Hubert being shown Miss Muffett by her father.

Annie H. has fun
seeing Little Orphan Annie.

Ashlee Moore enjoys her beautiful dress
before our photo shoot.

157 The Alfano family and their Young King Cole.

Chicago Pretender
A LITTLE BIT OF REALITY AND A LOT OF MAKE BELIEVE
Wolf Joins Chicago Fire Department
CHICAGO:
BREAKING NEWS –
Penelope Pig was just
rescued by her three
children and the Big Bad

Shadow's buddy, Tanzy, looks at the picture of herself and Shadow with Larry Broutman.

Special Dedication

My wife, Susan, and I joyfully dedicate this book to Shadow (2002-2018),
who gave unconditional love and so much more to the lives of all our family.
"Remembering Shadow" says it all.

Remembering Shadow

He was such a little peanut — we thought that should be his name,
and when he came into our lives we knew nothing would be the same.
We watched him very carefully, we watched him as he grew,
and after a very short time, there was something that we knew.

He followed Larry everywhere, he was always at his heel,
and so we had a change of heart 'cuz we began to feel
that Peanut wasn't apropos, and soon the time just came
to realize that Shadow was a much more perfect name.

The shadowing continued, he was always at Larry's feet,
and Larry loved this oh so much, for him it was a treat.
Shadow barked if Larry looked away, he wanted him every minute.
The two became the best of pals, there's no other way to spin it.

Shadow may not be here now, it's terribly sad to part,
but the memories will never fade, so deep in Larry's heart.

— *Sandy Horwitz*

Thanks

Much thanks to my wife, Susan, who was such a great help in posing some of the children. She was also very helpful in making suggestions as the illustrations were being developed by Rich Green.

Carol Haralson of Sedona, Arizona, award-winning book designer and text editor, has once more designed an amazing book. This is our fourth book together and quite a bit different from the last one, *Chicago Eternal*, a book based on my photographs from more than thirty Chicago cemeteries. Her wonderful poetic sensibility was so important here in creating modified nursery rhymes to accompany Rich Green's illustrations.

Sharon Woodhouse, publisher of Everything Goes Media/Lake Claremont Press and distributor of my first three books, will also distribute *Chicago Treasure*. Sharon has spent considerable time advising on our text, illustrations, and plans for distribution.

John Rabias, digital media expert and instructor at the School of the Art Institute of Chicago, helped to add whimsy to the book by combining my photographs of children with the photographs of iconic Chicago events and locations and also placing them into artworks for the "Now Showing!" gallery.

Lesley Wallerstein, an accomplished intellectual property attorney, reviewed the manuscript and advised on all matters relating to trademarks and copyrights.

Lee Burkland, principal of the Judy and Ray McCaskey Preschool Program at the Chicago Lighthouse for the Blind and Visually Disabled, made sure that all the children photographed at the school had received the approval of their parents. Lee also organized our photo shoots and made sure the priority was always first and foremost the children.

Sandy Horwitz, a wonderful writer and poet, made the poems she touched much better than my first attempts. Her loving poem for my buddy Shadow is so much appreciated. — LB

As with my previous books, all proceeds from sales of Chicago Treasure will be donated to two Chicago-based nonprofit service agencies: Access Living and The Chicago Lighthouse for People Who are Blind or Visually Impaired.

Index

Poems + Modified Nursery Rhymes

People, Places + Events

KEY TO THE PUZZLE ON PAGE 15

About the Authors

LARRY BROUTMAN, a native Chicagoan, was the first recipient of a doctorate degree in Plastics Engineering at MIT in Cambridge, Massachusetts. His professional life of teaching, research, and consulting in the industry was honored by election to the Plastics Hall of Fame. During a busy career, Larry also found time to pursue an interest in landscape and wildlife photography and to publish magazine articles devoted to those topics.

Larry began to photograph iconic Chicago locations when he was asked to create photomurals for the Ann & Robert H. Lurie Children's Hospital of Chicago. The resulting urbanscapes, whimsically inhabited by animals from Larry's wildlife imagery, adorn all the floors of the hospital. From this came his first book, *Chicago Unleashed*. Interest in photographing around Chicago led to Larry's next book, *Chicago Monumental*, in 2016. This one-of-a-kind collection, accompanied by informative text, forms a unique portrait of the city.

Larry's third book, *Chicago Eternal*, features photographs of sites and scenes from numerous cemeteries throughout the area, offering a further unusual view of the origins of his native city.

Currently in progress are *Chicago Courageous*, a pictorial history of heroic Chicagoans from all walks of life, and *African Treasure,* a book of Larry's African photography.

All author proceeds go to two Chicago-based nonprofit service agencies: The Chicago Lighthouse for People who are Blind or Visually Impaired, and Access Living.

RICH GREEN is an illustrator who can usually be found behind his computer imagining himself as the characters he draws to life. A former Disney intern, Rich graduated from Columbia College, Chicago with a focus on computer graphics. Although he works primarily digitally, he also enjoys putting pencil to paper or a brush into paint as well. Rich lives in Joliet, Ilinois, with his faithful dog Annie by his side as he creates.

Recently named Chicago-Area Illustrators Network Rep for the Society of Children's Book Writers and Illustrators, Rich has illustrated several popular children's books. He is also an executive board member of The Artist Guild of Lockport, and his personal artwork can be found in galleries and art exhibitions throughout the year.

JOHN RABIAS is a graphic artist who works in digital illustration and in post-production imaging to digitally manipulate images and retouch and color-correct photographs. For more than twenty years, he has been an instructor at the School of the Art Institute of Chicago teaching various computer applications, including Adobe Photoshop, Illustrator, and InDesign.

When not working digitally, John paints in oil. He lives in Chicago with his Gibson Les Paul and Fender Stratocaster.